THE WHISTLERS' ROOM

THE WHISTLERS' ROOM

by
Paul Alverdes

Translated by
Basil Creighton

Introduction by
Emily Mayhew

CASEMATE | uk

Oxford & Philadelphia

Published in Great Britain and
the United States of America in 2017 by
CASEMATE PUBLISHERS
The Old Music Hall, 106–108 Cowley Road, Oxford OX4 1JE, UK

and

1950 Lawrence Road, Havertown, PA 19083, USA

© Casemate Publishers 2017
Introduction © Emily Mayhew 2017
Series adviser: Elly Clark

Paperback Edition: ISBN 978-1-61200-466-2
Digital Edition: ISBN 978-1-61200-467-9 (epub)

A CIP record for this book is available from the British Library

Printed in the Czech Republic by FINIDR
Typeset in India by Lapiz Digital Services, Chennai

For a complete list of Casemate titles, please contact:

CASEMATE PUBLISHERS (UK)
Telephone (01865) 241249
Fax (01865) 794449
Email: casemate-uk@casematepublishers.co.uk
www.casematepublishers.co.uk

CASEMATE PUBLISHERS (US)
Telephone (610) 853-9131
Fax (610) 853-9146
Email: casemate@casematepublishing.com
www.casematepublishing.com

CONTENTS

INTRODUCTION

POINTNER, Kollin, Benjamin and Harry. The inhabitants of *The Whistlers' Room*. Four young men who have been soldiers fighting in the Great War. Each wounded in the throat, saved, and sent back to Germany. As a group confined by their casualty to a single hospital ward, sharing a prolonged, painful and uncertain journey towards recovery. In Paul Alverdes' remarkable novel of war and wounding, we will meet each of these souls individually, and hear their stories, and we will also come to understand the room – the world – that they inhabit, and the community they have made there. Alverdes will help us listen carefully to them, because the "Whistlers" speak in tones and a language that is so quiet and fragile, it is all too easily missed in the hubbub of war. But once we can hear it – hear them, we can never quite forget the sound.

In a review from 1930, the year of the publication of *The Whistlers' Room* in translation in Britain, The Spectator magazine said that it was "impossible to exaggerate the delicacy and originality of this piece of work." Additionally, it has a very particular power that comes from the writing in the novel being deeply rooted in a precise medical reality.

Alverdes was himself wounded in the throat, and it is clear that he paid very close attention to both his treatment and the treatment of others with a similar or more severe form of the same casualty. So the novel stands not just as an original and compelling artistic representation, it is also a valuable supplement to our understanding of the medical history of both the war and the period, both in Britain and in Germany. Weapons wounded just the same whichever side of the front they were fired from, and medics of all the combatant nations grew practised and expert at treating their consequences, as we shall see. In Britain, there were over sixty thousand soldiers who experienced damage to their face, jaw, throat and neck as a result of artillery shell fragments or high-velocity rifle bullets. Precise equivalent German casualty statistics are not easily determined but as all other forms of casualty were comparable with British figures or even higher, it is safe to assume that there were plenty of other patients for Alverdes to study alongside him on the ward.

One significant reason why these kinds of wounds were so prevalent was the nature of the evolution of war itself by 1914. In trench warfare, only the combatants' head and neck were exposed to the enemy, their bodies being protected by the trench itself. Metal helmets safeguarded the head (German helmets were considered to be the most effective at this) but the flesh of the face and the front of the neck was unprotected and therefore vulnerable, especially as troops charged forward into storms of shrapnel and artillery fragments. But they could also be inflicted at any time during a soldier's forward service at the front, not just during times of actual fighting in battle, particularly by sniper fire. Snipers were expertly trained and well-equipped with the latest high-velocity rifles which enabled them to fire an accurate and powerful shot from great distances. One of the first surgeons working to repair facial injuries in a hospital on the French coast, Charles Valadier, asked his patients why so many of them came to him after being hit by sniper fire. Snipers, he was told, always targeted what they thought was human flesh, rather than helmets or movement, because flesh reflected light in a different way to any other material, even when camouflaged in mud. Snipers learned to look for this particular reflection and to set it as their target, hence the great number of injuries to the flesh of the face and throat. Both sides used snipers throughout the war, and they were feared and despised in equal measure. It is notable that in the novel that, even though his own throat wound was inflicted by artillery shell fragments, Pointner has an English sniper's cap that he took from the battlefield where he was wounded, and that he refuses to give up no matter what (and that he keeps in the cupboard by his bed on the shelf where his chamber pot is stored).

From the outset, Alverdes takes care to emphasise that the Whistlers have been in their room for "a long while" – at least a year since their original wounding. By any measure, this is a long time to remain in hospital and it is a revealing detail about the complex nature of these wounds. Although it was initially assumed that someone shot in the throat would die, the military medical system quickly learned that this was not the case. Provided blood and debris from the wound could be kept away from the windpipe during evacuation (usually achieved by keeping the casualty sitting up rather than lying down on the stretcher as he was borne away by the bearers), these wounds were not immediately life-threatening in the same way that abdominal, head or chest wounds were. By 1916, throat and facial casualties could find themselves in the "lightly wounded" category for evacuation priorities. It was only in the next stage of medical treatment, in hospitals such as the one in the novel, that medical staff came to understand that there was never anything light about wounds to the face and throat. These injuries could be every bit as lethal as a chest or abdominal wound but they took life in their own way, slowly but surely, over months or years.

There were many factors at work in this process, but *The Whistlers' Room* is centred around one in particular where, as Alverdes puts it with his gentle precision: "the process of healing overshot its mark." The Whistlers are not just suffering from the same wound, but from the same physical complication that has confounded their recovery. Surgery has repaired the initial trauma but the repaired wound has had an abnormal healing response. Scar tissue, forming inside the windpipe itself, has grown larger than the original insult, narrowing the passage and thus changing the volume of air that they can inhale and exhale. Their ability to breathe normally is restricted to the point at which they are threatened with suffocation.

The medical term for the condition is tracheal stricture (sometimes tracheal stenosis) and it is primarily seen today following radiation therapy or tracheostomy or prolonged intubation – where a breathing tube has been inserted in the windpipe to maintain respiration artificially. As part of the healing response, tracheal stricture takes some time to develop, with patients awakening from surgery able to breathe normally. Then the medical condition known as stridor (abnormal, high-pitched, guttering breath sounds) develops as the windpipe is gradually and unstoppably blocked by scar tissue. Finally, breathing becomes difficult and oxygen supply to the body via the lungs insufficient. The condition is aggravated because abnormal scar development produces tissue architecture that is tougher, thicker and less flexible than normal skin tissue. Alverdes' description of this phenomenon is typically original, evocative, and medically precise: the internal scarring that deforms the Whistlers' windpipes is "tough … hardened like the bones of young children."

Treatment of tracheal stricture is the same today as it was a century ago in the operating theatre adjoining the Whistlers' ward. To provide immediate respiratory relief, a tracheotomy procedure is performed: surgically cutting a small hole in the neck below the level of the scarring and then inserting a tube with a vacuum fastening so that breathing air directly into the lungs can take place unimpeded. Instead of inhaling through the nose or mouth, the patient can now inhale through the tube and therefore receive sufficient oxygen. Only the material of the tube mechanism has changed. Today it is a medical-grade plastic but in the Whistlers' ward, each of them has had a small silver pipe inserted into his throat so he can breathe. Tracheotomy patients find it difficult to speak, but Alverdes tells us that his subjects have learned to manipulate the open end of their silver pipes so they can communicate with one another in their own specially evolved language of clicks and whistles to the extent that they can hold long, strange conversations with each other as the days and nights pass on their ward.

As an initial repair, the installation of silver pipes was effective but it was also the reason for their new owners' lengthy confinements. The pipe's exit point was an open wound, leading directly from the outside environment to the lungs. Even simple daily management to keep it clean and functional was difficult and complicated, and could only be done in a hospital. This was the pre-antibiotic era, and the risk of infection with throat and facial wounds was very high. The story of Benjamin's wounding gives insight into the filthy, chaotic environments that casualties were often left in before receiving hospital treatment. Gains made in treating wounds themselves were often confounded by the inability to master their accompanying or subsequent infections, which terrorised field hospital wards, as invisible and as deadly as snipers on the battlefield. Infections were just as hazardous to recovery in military hospitals at home. Every time the patient was fed or given liquids, the potential for food particles contaminating a wound so near the mouth or nose was significant. In the novel, Benjamin is given his first nutrition for days in the form of a drink – champagne, red wine, sugar and beaten egg. This was a standard mixture for such patients, and could also contain coffee and beef stock – protein, sugars in various forms, and alcohol for mood and as a muscle relaxants. The orderly who gave it to Benjamin would have been very skilled in administering the drink – any spillage would have been carefully cleaned up, so feeding could take hours. It was not just the risk of infection from foreign bodies. The feeding process was difficult and time-consuming, and every spoonful had to be ingested with great care. Patients who ended up coughing and spluttering could send food particles into their lungs. This risked causing pneumonia, which was almost always fatal in the case of wound-weakened physiologies. This condition is still feared today but, then as now, feeding of patients was essential if they were to regain strength not only for further treatment and resolution of their wounds, but also for the activities of daily living such as getting out of bed, walking and managing their own conditions as far as possible.

By the time we are introduced to the residents of *The Whistlers' Room*, we see the patients managing a certain amount of infection control themselves, without having to rely on nurses or orderlies unless they were bedridden. Alvardes' description is particularly poignant of both the pipe technology that enabled them to breath and the means by which it was kept clean, using clean white muslin fabric shields and specially made little round brushes. His emphasis on the material of the pipes sets the description in a particular emotional context. Silver is a precious metal, it is crafted into things by a silversmith, not in a factory, so there is something special and precious about these medical implements that allow their owners to breathe. There were also specific technical medical reasons why silver was used in these pipes. It has been known for centuries that, in addition to being easy to work into intricate designs and shapes, silver has antibacterial properties. Non-toxic to humans, silver not only resists bacterial growth on its surface, it actually disrupts it by limiting bacterial cell reproduction. It is used today in an increasing range of medical products (silver-lined sticking plasters, for instance) because in certain compounds, it not only resists bacteria, it actually promotes healing. Silver-imbedded medical equipment is also used in hospitals as part of the on-going efforts to combat superbugs.

Despite the Whistlers' pride in keeping themselves and their pipes clean, Alvardes is discreetly honest about the reality of their condition. Infections were never really eradicated, only managed up to a point – "the low fever never really left the whistlers" and Pointner has a serious form of septic blood poisoning. Small but precise details, such as those of the colouration of Pointner's nails and hands testify to the precarious nature of their survival. In the meantime, their reconstruction must continue. The silver pipes are only an intermediate treatment for their conditions. So the Whistlers receive regular surgical procedures to release their strictures and restore normal breathing. Their surgeon works "to widen by degrees their natural air channel … by insertions of sharp spoons and tongs" and rods "forced past the constricted passage of the throat." Eventually the throat will be sufficiently widened so that the pipes can be removed, the external wound closed up, and normal breathing be resumed. This element of treatment has also not changed a great deal a century on. Surgeons perform dilation procedures which seek to stretch out the scar tissue and widen the trachea. They use surgical dilators (a type of surgical scissor with a rounded end) or small balloons which can be inserted down a tube and then gently inflated to stretch and smooth out the surrounding tissue. Whilst the technique may be the same across the century, there is one significant and especially brutal difference: today tracheal stricture relief is done under general anaesthetic, but for the Whistlers it was not.

There were many fields of medical practice that were greatly advanced by their application and repeated practice in warfare, but anaesthetics was not among them. It was not really considered to be a medical procedure at all, but a non-professional trade that supported surgery. It would not become an "ology" until the interwar period, fully medicalised, with proper training and the beginnings of a research infrastructure. Throughout the Great War anaesthetics were dangerous and deeply unpleasant – the slightest whiff of chloroform or ether enough to make patients vomit or weep in terror as they waited outside operating theatres. Anaesthetic gases were administered via face masks in a bludgeoning dose of chemicals, and great care had to be taken as the patient's breathing and blood pressure was depressed. Worst of all was the altered mental state of the patient which could result in extreme writhing or jerking movements, making delicate surgery all but impossible. Georges Duhamel, in his classic work of military medicine set in France during the Great War, *The New Book of Martyrs* wrote of the "disorderly intoxication, the muscular animal rebellion of those who are thrown into this artificial sleep." If the injury or patient could not tolerate the gas mask, then default delivery method was ether in solution administered rectally. Some injuries complicated the delivery of anaesthetics beyond practicality or risk, tracheal stricture being one of them. It was next to impossible to operate on a patient's face or throat if a gas mask was in use, and the surgeon performing the procedure would need to be able to hear the patient's breathing at all times to know that he was not impeding it more than necessary. Additionally, aggravated movement of the kind Duhamel described could be fatal, so for all of these reasons, the Whistlers endured "the healing torture" of their surgical repairs awake and without pain medication of any kind.

For them to do so, required a surgeon who inspired their confidence, and Alverdes describes Doctor Quint, who treats the Whistlers in strong characterising detail so that we understand why they trust him so. He is a physically imposing man who rarely shouts, but when he does, the Whistlers feel a certain pride in knowing that the voice resounding authoritatively through the hospital belongs to their surgeon. He generates a competitive but communal spirit amongst his patients, who he treats as a group, "three in a row on a long bench, wrapped in white sheets up to the chin." Each of them understands better than anyone else in the world what the other is going through, so that whatever they are suffering, isolation is not one of its features. In the Second World War, surgeon Archibald McIndoe sought to generate the same kind of communal treatment ethos in his patients who had been badly burned in the Royal Air Force. They became known as "The Guinea Pig Club" and attended each other's operations, giving each other support and advice on rehabilitation techniques and pain management – all of it prefigured by the story of the world of the Whistlers' room.

Alvardes gives Quint very particular features that tell us of another community beyond the war, struggling not to be changed by it. Quint wears "an English suit" – his style of dress with silk socks and patent leather shoes might be seen to be that of a quintessential English gentleman in Saville Row tailoring. But this is not simply a question of personal style. By 1916 it was no longer acceptable in war-wracked Germany to demonstrate an affinity with anything English so Quint's personal obstinacy is notable. Links between the British, German and Austrian medical professions at all levels were very strong. The generation of surgeons and clinicians who had graduated in the first decade of the twentieth century sought out fellowships in each other's countries, spending a year in London or Vienna or Berlin as surgical or clinical residents. They spoke each other's languages (something that would come in particularly useful when dealing with each other's prisoners of war on the front). They read and wrote for each other's journals. These connections were strongly maintained right up until the last weeks of peace in 1914 (they even went to each other's conferences in the early months of the summer). Perhaps Quint's insistence on his English tailoring is his attempt to signal that there is still life in the pan-European medical community above and beyond the war.

There are other details in the novel that speak to the commonality of the experience of war and wounding across nations. We learn from Pointner's treatment after he is wounded that German casualties were welcomed and "beflowered" by the civilian population. Dusseldorf Station, one of the primary processing points for German casualties, was decorated throughout with arrangements of flowers, kept watered and replaced when necessary by volunteers, just as they were in Charing Cross Station in London or Birmingham New Street. In the streets outside the stations, flowers were strewn in the paths of ambulances driving out to the hospitals, or handed in to the patients themselves through the windows. The medical staff who accompanied their patients found this behaviour inconvenient (cigarettes were much more welcome) but some patients had a few brief moments of enjoyment as the flowers were handed to them and patriotic songs rang out as they finally found themselves at home.

*

As we grow accustomed to the world in the Whistlers' room, Alverdes introduces a new patient whose story is perhaps the strangest of all. Furlein has no physical wound yet he too has returned from the Front unable to speak – "it was an effort for him to produce even a hoarse whisper" – and he has difficulty breathing. Furlein's is one of a range of conditions relating to speech. He is probably suffering from aphonia (inability to talk above a whisper), but similar military casualties also were diagnosed with psychogenic dysphonia (inability to speak loudly) or functional mutism (inability to speak at all). All of them are specific forms of what is now called post traumatic stress disorder (PTSD), but which in 1916 went by a variety of different names, including shell shock, neurasthenia, or mental shock. During the First World War, thousands of German casualties of this kind poured into military hospitals on the front and at home. Many were admitted to the Department of Psychiatric and Nervous Disorders at the Charité Hospital in Berlin. There were two schools of thought amongst specialists treating these patients. Some believed that the breakdowns had been triggered by incidents at the war itself: a kind of traumatic neurosis. Others identified their patients as having "a psychopathic constitution" which predisposed them to hysteria. By 1917, this became the dominant discourse, with a range of therapies designed to help the patient recover their disordered nervous system and physical functions.

Electro-therapy was one frequently a treatment option for such disorders. The chief proponent for its use in treating aphonia was Richard Hirschfeld at the Charité, and he devised both a technological and diagnostic system that was adopted across the profession. Electrotherapy comprised the application of an electric current of varying strength to the part of the body affected by loss of function, for between two and five minutes, sometimes accompanied by exercises or hypnosis before a return to the current's application. The current was applied using a Faradic brush: an electrode embedded into a long-insulated handle that attached to a small generator. The electrode's end was made of densely packed, nickel-plated copper wire bristles, that delivered currents of electricity when applied to the dry skin of the body directly in brief strokes or taps. Recovery rates were generally said to be high although there were few outcome studies that looked to see if functional problems returned after treatment. It is this treatment that Quint uses on Furlein, rather than sending him on to a more appropriate institution, but it is not the only one. Several weeks before he fires up the generator, and applies the brushes to the patient's non-functioning throat, Quint recognises the Whistlers' own expertise by immersing Furlein in the therapeutic community of the Whistlers' room itself where, in some of the most tender scenes of the entire novel, its more permanent inhabitants can care for him in their own unique ways.

*

We meet the fourth Whistler late in the novel. Unexpectedly, he is an English prisoner of war named Harry Flint. Flint has also been shot in the throat and transferred to the ward from a prisoner-of-war camp hospital. Although this seems unusual, the treatment of seriously injured prisoners of war in specialist medical units in Germany was not uncommon. London's Imperial War Museum holds an archive for one such patient, whose history has particular similarities to that of Harry Flint. James Grey, of the Middlesex Regiment, was injured in the very opening days of the war, in August 1914. He was shot in the face during the retreat from Mons, captured, and spent the few months shuttling around the prisoner-of-war camp hospital network in increasingly desperate attempts to cope with his casualty. He could only consume liquid broth and was unable to speak. Finally, weakened and close to death, he was sent for treatment at Germany's leading hospital for jaw injuries, the Westdeutsche Kieferklinik in Dusseldorf.

Grey's archive is small but contains one fascinating artefact – a photograph album full of images taken whilst he was a patient in the Klinik. Text from the novel might easily be applied as captions for the photographs. We see Grey wearing "the hospital uniform of blue and white striped linen, and over it a kind of round cape" that is described in Alverdes' story. On his head was a washed-out cap of the same material just as Harry wears. Grey must also have earned the trust of his wardmates, as Harry tries to do in the novel. The album shows images of him alongside his German counterparts in his bed on the ward and then, as he was treated and grew stronger, in his striped uniform out in the garden of the Klinik, walking or seated together on a bench. The archive also tells us that Grey's German became good enough for him to help patients from the nearby ward for the blind with walks in to the garden (just as Benjamin does with Deuster) and to read their letters to them.

The Klinik has other similarities to the hospital in Alverdes' novel. It is set in beautiful cultivated grounds of a mature garden and tall trees, with a view of the Rhine in the distance. The two consultants who were its medical directors, Christian Bruhn and August Lindemann, conceived it as a specialist facial repair hospital, with the expectations that their patients would be there for long periods of time, for both treatment and rehabilitation. They were intolerant of the military authorities who ran the hospital, and both had international reputations of which they were justly proud. They spoke excellent English, and so were able to explain to Grey the exact nature and treatment of his injuries in his own language. Lindemann was cited throughout the war by British surgeons, such as Harold Gillies, as fundamental to the development of the surgical repair of facial wounds. After the war, as Surgeon Quint would have been reassured to know, German experts such as Lindemann were able to re-establish their relationships with their international counterparts, at least until the degradation of the German medical community by the policies of the Nazi regime, begun in 1933.

*

Not all medical treatment or infrastructure was the same in both Britain and Germany. In a brief but fascinating aside, Alverdes notes a difference between the reaction of Harry and Benjamin to their being referred to the skin clinic portion of the hospital, known as "The Ritterburg." They are both suffering from skin conditions that (as a result of the scabies mite) are causing their skin to break out in itchy, painful and contagious lesions. What puzzles Harry (and perhaps the novel's British readership) is that Benjamin feels great shame in being transferred to the skin clinic for treatment. Since medieval times, German medicine was structured so that venereal diseases and skin conditions were combined as one specialty. (This continues to be the case in some continental European countries where consultants may certify in dermato-venereology.) Because of this structure, the shame and subsequent ostracizing of venereal disease patients also attached itself to those suffering from skin conditions, and the visible marks of dermatological conditions accrued a similar moral dimension – sin on the inside manifesting in exterior signs. (The term "Ritterburg" means a knight's castle – a fortified place where sufferers were contained or imprisoned, where their treatment was also a form of punishment – a very different ethos from the Whistlers' room.)

*

So, for Harry, and especially for Benjamin, there is relief to be back in their own world of the Whistlers' room, amongst their own kind, with its gentle rhythms and language, and once again the view of the trees and the Rhine in the distance. But time passes, and their recovery remains slow and fragile. Winter comes, and snow. A regimental band plays rousing patriotic tunes outside their window. Then, quickly, in sudden steps, everything in their world changes. Alverdes ends the story here, almost as the echoes of the bugles and drums of the band fade away in the cold air of the garden. All that is left to us as we close the book are the memories of the slight, quiet silver piping of the Whistlers forever in their room. This, I think, is as it should be. Alverdes has delivered a message as essential then as it is now. When the blasts and crashes of war are over, we must remember to listen for the sights and sounds of those lives forever changed, who speak in whispers of the world of pain to which they too are confined.

Emily Mayhew
London, 2017.

DEDICATED

TO

HANS CAROSSA

I

THE large room with the wide terrace in front and the view over the park and fields and a glimpse of the Rhine in the distance beneath a brown cloud of smoke was known throughout the hospital as the Whistlers' Room. It was named after the three soldiers who had been shot in the throat and awaited their recovery there. They had been there a long while; some said since the first year of the war. The stretcher-bearers who were the first to bandage them under fire in the shelter of ruined houses or in dugouts roofed over with planks and turf, pronounced on them a sentence of speedy death; but in defiance of all precedent and expectation they came through, for the time at any rate.

The process of healing, however, overshot its mark: for the bullet holes were covered over on the inner side of the windpipe by new flesh in such thick rolls and weals that the air passage was speedily blocked, and a new channel had to be made to meet this unforeseen threat of suffocation. So the surgeon's knife cut a small hole in the neck below the old wound, which was causing a more and more impassable block. At this point a tube was sunk into the windpipe, and the air then passed freely in and out of the lungs.

The tube was a small silver pipe of the length and thickness of the little finger. At its outer end there was a small shield, fixed at right angles, not larger than the identity disc that everyone at the front wore next his skin. The purpose of it was to prevent the tube slipping into the gullet; and to prevent it falling out, there was a white tape passing through two eye-holes in the shield and secured behind round the neck by a double slip knot. In fact, however, the pipe was of two parts, closely fitted together, the innermost of which was held in its place by a tiny winged screw. Three times a day it was pulled out by two small handles to be cleaned; for since they could not now breathe through the nostrils, the tubes had become as it were the whistlers' noses, and when they were not actually bedridden they gladly cleaned them for themselves with the little round brush provided for that purpose.

After it was cleaned the entrance of the tube had at once to be protected against dust and flies by a clean curtain. This was about the size of the hand and rectangular in form. It was cut from a thick roll of white muslin and attached to the tape with pins. It recalled the clerical band that forms part of the official garb of evangelical clergymen. Thus it was that the whistlers, with their spotless white between chin and chest, had always a ceremonial air. They were well aware of it. There was something of this in their whole bearing, and gladly they changed their bibs and tuckers several times a day for even cleaner and whiter ones. When they breathed quickly or laughed, a soft piping note, like the squeaking of mice, came from the silver mouth. Hence they were called the neck whistlers, or the whistlers simply.

Talking, after being for a long while practically dumb, gave them great trouble at first, and they were glad to avoid it, particularly before strangers. When they wished to speak they had to close the mouth of the pipe with the tip of the finger. Then a thread-like stream of air found its way upwards through the throat and played on the vocal cords, or what remained of them; and they, very unwillingly roused from their torpor, emitted no more than a painful wheezing and croaking.

It was not, however, for their cracked notes that the whistlers blushed, but for this to-do with lifting their bibs and feeling with their fingers for their secret mouthpiece; and this predicament they tried every means to disguise. Were a stranger to address them on the roads through the park, or in the wide passages and halls of the great building where in bad weather they sometimes took their walks, they usually forbore returning an immediate answer. They looked in meditation down at their toes, or with head courteously inclined and raised eyebrows gazed into the face of him who accosted them as though earnestly seeking within themselves for a suitable response. Meanwhile, quite without any particular object, they put up a hand to their breasts and after a moment proceeded as though to dally with a shirt button that might be concealed beneath the white pinafore. After this they began to talk and sometimes, if they gained sufficient confidence, their first silence might be exchanged for a cheerful loquacity. It was as though they wished to show that, in the very natural and, indeed, most everyday matter of being hoarse, they were not any different from other men. Why they did this they could not themselves have said; and they did not speak of it to each other. Yet they all behaved as though sworn to secrecy by oath; and when a fourth was added to them, he, from the very first, did likewise.

It was just the same, moreover, with the others in the room upstairs who had lost an arm or a leg. They felt no shyness at being seen by strangers with an empty sleeve or a trouser leg dangling loose and empty; indeed some of them vaunted their docked limbs and even went so far as to instil a kind of grizzly veneration in those who had come off more lightly by a display of their sad stumps. Yet the scraping and creaking of the sometimes not very successful appliances with which they had to learn to walk again, caused them acute embarrassment before strangers. At once they came to a stop and tried to disguise the grasp for the lever that enabled them to fix the artificial joint by catching or pulling at their trousers, or by any other apparently trivial movement. They never, either, displayed an unclothed false hand or foot, and at night when they undressed for bed they concealed the arm they had screwed off by hanging the coat over it, or the leg by leaving it carefully in a corner inside the trouser. For they were always afraid of being surprised by outsiders, and would have liked best being always by themselves.

Sometimes, however, visitors from outside came to distribute gifts—to the whistlers as well in their room.

They made presents of wine, fruit and cakes, and especially of all kinds of scent with which the whistlers gladly and copiously besprinkled themselves. It is true that their sense of smell was for the time in abeyance; but they were all the more gratified to feel that they carried a pleasant aroma about with them. For all that, these occasions of munificence did not long continue. For too often the visitors came to a hasty conclusion that he who could not utter a sound, or only in a treble voice, must necessarily be stone deaf as well, and they proceeded to shout at the whistlers without mercy; and some even pulled out notebooks and wrote in enormous letters what they might just as well have said; or they tried from the very outset to make themselves intelligible by gestures of the most exaggerated description. For the whistlers this was gross insult. The defect which they had now adopted as a peculiarity of their own, seemed to them in a sense a merit, and no longer really a defect at all. But the one that was thus falsely laid to their door wounded them to the quick. And so, no sooner had the unknown visitor entered at one door than they took flight by another. But if they were caught in bed they pretended to be asleep, or put their fingers warningly to their lips, shook their heads with a pretence of regret, and enjoined upon the intruders an alarmed and guilty retreat.

Among themselves the whistlers held lively and intimate talks. They could do so easily in a wordless clucking speech that, in default of a stream of air to make words with, they formed by means of their lips and tongues and teeth. Their powers of comprehension had arrived at such a pitch that in the night, when lights were out and when there was no help from gestures of the hands, they held long talks between three from bed to bed. It sounded like the incessant clucking and splashing in a water-butt under the changing quick patter of heavy drops. For the low fever that seldom left the whistlers, or the effect of the drugs they were given, kept them often long awake. They never talked of a future and seldom of a past before the war. But of their last day at the front and of the exact circumstances in which they were wounded they never tired of giving vivid and stirring accounts; and with such leisure for recollection there was always more and more to add, and sometimes, indeed, an entirely new story was evolved and told for the first time. But not one of them showed any surprise at that.

I I

THERE was one thing, however, to be told of the eldest of the three that could not be varied, and this was that a shell splinter had smashed his jaws and his larynx. His name was Pointner, and he was a peasant's son from Bavaria. He had been for over a year in the whistlers' room, and his case was the worst of the three. He had got blood-poisoning and slowly, almost imperceptibly, his condition became hopeless. He often had to be in bed, with a high temperature, and then there was little he could be tempted to eat. Though well grown and well nourished when he left home, he was now as lank as a young boy. But nothing vexed him so much as when some of the convalescents from other wards picked him up like a child in their arms and offered to carry him about. A dark flush came into his cheeks, and he spat and scratched in rage and hit out unsparingly on all sides with his fever-wasted hands. He was ashamed of weighing so little. Nobody who saw him now would have guessed that he had been a butcher by trade, a master of all the secrets of the slaughter-house and an adept at making sausages. To be sure his time for that was over.

Perhaps Pointner had been once of a hot-blooded and even truculent disposition. He had a photograph of himself as a reservist on the cupboard beside his bed in a highly decorated frame of silver metal. This frame was composed of two gnarled oak trees, whose branches, through which ran broad scrolls bearing inscriptions, were gathered together along the top and bore the crown of a princely house; at their base amid the mighty roots was entwined a bunch of all kinds of swords, flags, rifles and cavalry lances. Between the oaks, however, reservist Pointner was to be seen, his cap, beneath which a love-lock protruded, set rakishly over one ear, and two fingers of the right hand stuck between the buttons of his tunic. In his left was jauntily held a cane bound with a plaited band from which depended a knot. His jaw was unusually strong and prominent, and this gave an aggressive turn to his short stature and the amiable expression of the upper part of his face. "Reserve now has rest," was written on the photograph, and it was lightly tinted in bright colours. Nevertheless reserve had not had rest and the aggressive jaw had disappeared, and a small boneless and retreating chin had taken its place. It gave his face, with the always slightly parted lips and the white gleam of the upper teeth—which had escaped unscathed—beneath the straw-coloured moustache, a childlike and weak expression. And indeed the alteration in Pointner was more and more marked, though the old hot blood still sometimes came uppermost and made him dangerous.

Pointner had been wounded in one of the first fights with the English, and after that had lain for a week or two in a field hospital. From there one morning he found his way, in the midst of a crowd of lightly wounded cases, and quite contrary to regulations, into an emergency hospital train and got back to Germany. He was clothed in a long-skirted hospital garment of blue and white striped cotton, with felt slippers on his feet. On his head he wore an English sniper's cap, which he had brought with him on the stretcher as booty and had never surrendered. Speechless as he was, with face and neck bandaged up to the eyes, and with no papers either, he was taken for an English prisoner throughout the journey and treated as such. Even the memory of this threw him into a rage. Certainly, the simplest thing would have been to cast away the khaki cap, but to this he could not bring himself. Rather than that he remained a Britisher in his own despite, passed over unwelcomed and unbeflowered, and left on one side in his stretcher shedding tears of rage. It was not till later that he succeeded in making himself understood.

Nevertheless, in spite of peremptory orders, he still kept the cap safely in a lower shelf of the cupboard which served as the retreat for a different article. Now and then when neither doctor nor nurse was expected to come in, he took it out. With care he polished the badge and the chin strap till they shone, and had a long look at it, turning it about meanwhile in his delicate hands, where the whites of the nails were turning from snow white to a bluish tinge.

I I I

KOLLIN, the second whistler, was a volunteer and Prussian pioneer. He had round and very bright blue eyes, set close together in a thin long face, and a hooked nose that increased its air of fearlessness. Kollin suffered keenly under his disablement, for he was ambitious and had set his heart on promotion. He often examined his wound with despairing impatience in a little pocket-mirror, and angrily shook his head when compelled to find that there was no alteration to be seen. Many a morning, after dreaming that he was cured, he woke to find himself entirely recovered and free from his disablement. He seemed to breathe freely again in the normal way, and got up at once to prove it to his comrades with his eyes shining. But it did not last long. Even before the doctor's visit he had to admit that his breath began to fail him, and that everything was as before.

Kollin's passion was numbers and number games. In warm weather, too, he sat all day long outside on the terrace with Pointner, bent over the chessboard and surrounded by a group of silent spectators. He hung a long while over each move, and as he hovered with slightly trembling hands over the board, he seemed to be cogitating a second game in the recesses of his mind. Now and again he made notes on a piece of paper. Pointner, whose moves were made with rapidity and who loved to rap down his pieces with a smart report, looked out meanwhile over the park as though bored and indifferent. He made himself acquainted with the alteration on the board without more than a lightning glance over his shoulder; but all the same his flushed cheeks grew darker as the threat of checkmate drew nearer and nearer. He still, however, made a few more moves with a hand as light as though they followed of themselves; and a disdainful and superior gesture made it very clear that reservist Pointner was not to be caught so simply. He would have dearly liked now and then to whistle a tune just to show that he had every reason to be content, but he was no more able to whistle than the other whistlers; but at least he could purse up his lips to show that he meant to, and produce a tiny sound that recalled the cheery chirp of a finch. Even while he did so he was already avoiding the eyes of the onlookers, who were unable any longer to hide their glee over the progress of the game. Suddenly, when Kollin was about to draw the noose tighter and turn his careful preparations into leisurely triumph, he broke out. With short round movements from the wrist, like the pats of a cat, he sent the pieces flying in all directions. At the same time, reddening with anger and shame, he got up with a final contemptuous gesture to signify he would have no more of it, pulled his cap down over his fair hair, and stumped off into the park without looking round. Kollin smiled grimly and shrugged his shoulders.

Then he gathered up the chessmen and put them back as they were, in order to demonstrate to the onlookers that the inevitable progress of the game could not have ended otherwise than in his own conclusive victory. But usually they, too, had lost interest and gone away one after another, leaving Kollin alone with his aggrieved reflections. Pulling out his notebook he wrote down exactly how the game had gone. "White," he wrote, and then in brackets: "Reservist Pointner gives up." After his death there was found among his papers an exact account of every game played in the whistlers' room. In the course of two years he had played fifteen hundred and eighty-nine games, and of these he had won seven hundred and one. The rest had been broken off by his opponent in desperate straits.

The next morning, at latest, after a game had been broken off in this way, Pointner always set out the chessboard before breakfast had even been brought in, and sat waiting in silence beside it. Kollin meanwhile went on reading an old newspaper; but soon he was unable to endure the pleasures of anticipation or to attend to what he read, and laying the paper aside he silently took his seat at the board. Sometimes on such mornings Pointner prevailed on himself to sit out his defeat.

I V

THE third whistler, a boy of seventeen, was called Benjamin. He had been christened so in a field hospital close up to the line on the west front. One October morning, just as it was getting light, a so-called char-à-banc arrived there. It was a vehicle with two long benches opposite each other, the whole enclosed within a square covering of grey tent-cloth that came closely down on all sides. As could be seen, it belonged to a Westphalian battery which had been put out of action the day before.

For a moment nothing stirred. Then a man without a tunic, in mud-caked breeches, climbed down backwards and very circumspectly out of the caravan. Last came his left arm, bent up to the level of his chest in a superfluously large makeshift splint. "Vice-Quartermaster Joseph," he reported to the doctor who at that moment came out of the entrance with sleeves rolled up and a brown rubber apron over his white overalls. "Vice-Quartermaster Joseph, of so-and-so regiment, with eleven severely wounded men of his battery."

These eleven sat dazed and fevered, or hung rather, with sunken heads, since there was no room to lie, along both benches inside the char-à-banc. Some clung fast to each other, and none moved when the covering was thrown back and the bearers came up with stretchers. One after another they were carried out. The last was a boy who, as he was carried in, his blood-stained coat on the arms of an immense Army Medical Corps non-commissioned officer, suddenly cheered up and tried to say something. Meanwhile he described wide circles with his hands across the sky which now began to show its cloudless blue, and raised his eyebrows and blew out his cheeks; he seemed, too, to wish to convey certain numbers. But not a sound proceeded from his throat. "To be sure," said the doctor in a deep quiet voice, laying a finger gently under his chin, "to be sure, it is Joseph and his brethren, and you must certainly be Benjamin. I'll put you all together in the best ward we have."

None the less they were no sooner in their beds than they began dying. On the very same day five of Joseph's brethren were wound in the sheets they could warm no longer and carried out. But the boy was called Benjamin from then onwards.

And next it seemed that he, too, would never get back to Germany. The doctor forbade him meat or drink. But during the night the house in which they were was set on fire by a shell from a long-range gun, and Benjamin, who lay under a blanket on his palliasse, was strapped on a stretcher and taken out naked—for the unexpected stream of wounded that day had exhausted the supply of nightshirts. In this manner he reached another house, but owing to the disorder that followed upon the sudden shelling and the outbreak of fire, the prohibition did not catch him up even on the next day. Thirst tortured him, and with raised hands he begged a cup of the soup that was being taken round to the rest of the room. He had scarcely attempted to swallow a sip of it before he felt as though someone gripped him by the throat with both hands. In horror he sprang right up out of bed and tore his mouth open as far as it would go. But do as he might—throwing his head about on all sides with his chest convulsively distended, and striking out at last with arms and shoulders as though swimming in the water, and turning wildly round and round where he stood—he could not succeed in inhaling the least breath of air. Finally, while his comrades shouted for help, he raged over and over on his bed without uttering a sound, and then rising once more to his feet fell forward senseless.

Often he told the whistlers in after days how he stormed death with all the strength of his soul and actually reached his goal. There, at a stroke, he had lost all desire for breath, and, hovering without weight in the void, had felt light and airy as he never felt before in his whole life. At the same time music rang out in a melody that he could never convey; but certainly no musician in the world could ever hit on notes like those. After that, he would conclude, he might well say it was good to die. The whistlers listened with earnest faces and nodded their heads; they did not doubt it. To anyone else Benjamin never said a word of all this; nor of all that he still had to go through in that hospital.

He was awoken by sudden merciless pain. At once the music ceased and his agony returned; but just as he tried to renew his struggles the cool air streamed like water into his lungs. He began to breathe once more, and once more felt that he had weight and was lying on his back; and this, too, he felt as a happiness.

Later he was told that the doctor happened to be on his way to visit other cases nearby, and hurrying in at the cries for help, arrived in the nick of time to catch Benjamin in his arms. As he had not his case of instruments with him he had pierced Benjamin's throat with his pocket knife.

After this Benjamin began to recover very quickly. But it seemed that his being still had a hankering after the experience that had already cost so dear. One morning, not long afterwards, just as the doctor attended by his orderlies was carefully cleaning the wound, the artery on the left side of the throat burst, as though it had been too long dammed, and shot the blood in a crimson arch out of his mouth. The vein had been severed by the bullet, but a piece of sinewy flesh which had likewise been shot through had clapped itself like a piece of plaster over the torn artery and for the time arrested the flow of blood.

Benjamin was beyond all terror as the hot torrent surged over his hands that he put up in astonishment to catch it. He looked into the doctor's face. Then he felt himself bent down backwards, and while his head hung down over the edge of the table the knife began burrowing after the vein in his extended throat. Meanwhile, at every beat of the heart, the blood was forced up like a pulsing fountain and fell back on his face, blinding his eyes with a gleaming scarlet veil. But the effect was to make him feel more and more light-headed, and the faint click of the needle, as he was stitched up, made an almost cheerful impression on him. It sounded like the clicking of knitting needles and caused him no pain. Then it ceased and the blood, too, came to a stop. A sponge was passed lightly over his eyes; he was slowly raised up and saw before him the doctor's white face, bespattered with blood right to the roots of his beard. He held an instrument of shining steel in his hand, and playfully pinched Benjamin's nose with it. "Well," he said quietly, "there you are again, my son."

Towards midday, however, Benjamin began to be very much afraid. He opened his eyes wide, yet he was unable to read the name-plate at the head of the bed opposite, though it was quite near and inscribed with large white letters on a black ground. He took this as a warning of death. Pulling his sheet over his head he prayed with hands together. After that for a long while he wept. Towards evening he felt slightly better; he wrote on a piece of paper asking if he would ever get better, and gave it to the orderly when he came with a drink for him. But the orderly made no answer; he only put his hand silently behind his back and the cup to his lips. It was a mixture of champagne, red wine, sugar and beaten egg.

V

FIVE weeks later he was driven through the park in a cab and stopped in front of the building in which was the whistlers' room. On his head he had a cap without a badge, and he was clothed in a tattered tunic that was far too big for him. It had been given him for his journey to Germany. In addition he wore trousers of brown corduroy with a red piping. There were flowers in his buttonhole. He smelt very strongly of eau-de-Cologne, and he felt a little uneasy over it. For as he refused the cigars that the ladies pressed upon him in the station and also might not eat or drink, they insisted at least upon refreshing his face with sponges dipped in eau-de-Cologne. He did not like to resist, and as he was dumb and had to sit for half an hour with the other wounded soldiers in a long row on the platform till the cabs came, this refreshment was repeated time after time by one lady after another.

It was Backhuhn who opened the door for him and helped him to alight. Backhuhn was a Silesian grenadier. A crossing shot had taken off his nose, and the doctors were in course of making him a new one by a recently devised method. To this end they had to start by grafting on the spot a few pieces of his own flesh with the skin and hair belonging to it. This superstructure had been incorporated most satisfactorily, and even beyond expectation, as they said, but for the time it was painful to look at, for it was as big as his two fists and towered up far beyond his forehead. In form and colour it resembled a fowl prepared for the oven, and hence the noseless grenadier had been given the name Backhuhn, or the roasting fowl. He was delighted with the name, for he was proud of the pains the doctor took over him, and wore his disfigurement as though it were a sort of decoration. From time to time he underwent a surgical operation, and the design was brought nearer to completion by stages that were often scarcely appreciable. Between whiles he was allowed to go about as he pleased.

Backhuhn loved to slip up behind the servant girls of the clinic and to cover their eyes with his hands. Then he asked them who it was, and if they could not guess, he turned them swiftly about. "Do you like me? Can you bear me?" he asked them in his gurgling voice and grinned in their faces.

Often they cried out in horror, threw up their hands and ran away. He, however, was delighted and sprang after them with uncouth gestures; and, in spite of all, they all got fond of him by degrees, for he was very big and tall, and he tried to make himself agreeable whenever he found an opportunity by his immense strength which was quite unimpaired.

For a long while it was one of his privileges to greet new arrivals and conduct them in or help to carry them.

He could not understand it at all when at last he had to be stopped; for he confidently expected the best results from the sight he presented, and never neglected to make them a little speech bearing thereon.

"Look at me, comrade," he said on this occasion to Benjamin, as he lifted him from the carriage. "I had no nose left, not as much as that, my boy, but now it's all right. They give you back here whatever you've lost."

Benjamin was glad to have someone to help him along, for he could only walk with difficulty; and in this way he reached the bathroom where all newcomers were first taken.

He felt embarrassed when he caught sight there of two nurses in long washing aprons with their sleeves rolled up, who were apparently waiting for him. For he had never known what it was to be given helplessly over to the hands of women for all that he needed doing to him. Also he was suddenly conscious that his whole body was caked with dirt and dried blood. He had been brought in in mud-soaked clothing, and, among so many severely wounded and dying cases, no one had had time to give him more than a hasty cleaning up. He was glad now he had not resisted the plentiful sprinklings of eau-de-Cologne on his arrival at the station, and expected every minute to see a bath orderly come along to relieve the nurses. But when these two put him on a chair and without ceremony began to undress him, a blush of shame overspread his face. At the same time he had the most intense longing to explain the pickle they would find him in. He kept fast hold of his trousers with both hands when the younger of the two tried to pull them from his legs, and began addressing her in his voiceless fashion. Unfortunately she could not understand him, and no more could the other when, at his increasing signs of embarrassment, she held her ear close to his lips. Meanwhile they were not at all discouraged and made various joking guesses at his meaning; but to each he replied with despairing gestures. At length they assured him that they understood him and skipped laughing out of the room and came back again pushing in front of them a chair on wheels with a lid on its box-shaped seat. Benjamin turned away and shook his head; he was almost in tears. After that he let himself be undressed and hoisted into the tub without another word. They buckled a kind of chest-strap round him, like those that children learn to walk with, so that he should not fall this way and that, and then soaped and washed him, talking all the while and laughing at his weight. They put their warm hands pityingly round his poor little arms, as they called them, and told off the vertebræ of his spine and each of his ribs with the tips of their fingers. Benjamin, however, for very confusion made no response. Obediently he held out arms and legs and bent his back to be scrubbed just as they required of him and gave himself up to them like a dumb animal. After that they enveloped him in a warmed shirt, and putting him on a wheeled stretcher took him down the long corridor to the whistlers' room. Kollin and Pointner were waiting for him at the open door, and Benjamin saw with delight that they, too, like him, had tubes in their necks.

V I

THE whistlers loved one another; not that they would have admitted it to themselves or displayed their feelings to each other. But every time, as often happened, one of them was wheeled away on a stretcher to submit to the knife and forceps of the surgeon, the two who remained could play no game and hold no talk. Instead they busied themselves on the floor with one thing and another, each by himself, and went again and again, as though for no particular reason, as far as the big swing doors that separated the corridor from the operating theatre. At last the stretcher came trundling back, looking now like a white model of a mountain, for over the recumbent figure was now the arc light, a kind of wooden tunnel with many lamps inside, whose purpose was to warm the patient during his return. They walked along beside him as though at a christening, or, indeed, at a funeral. They cautiously lifted the cloth from his face that protected it from the draught and nodded and winked as though to say: "We three know what it is, and no one else does but us." And the returning one, in spite of his pain, nodded back.

At that time the doctor was doing his best to widen by degrees the whistlers' natural air channel so that one day they would be able to breathe without pipes. It was done by repeated insertions of sharp spoons and tongs, and at last by pushing in long nickel rods and forcing them past the constricted passage of the throat. The process was, in fact, exactly the same as stretching gloves with glove stretchers, and, since it had to be carried out without an anæsthetic, it caused the whistlers the most acute pain. For it seemed that nature wished to protect from further interference what had once been torn without its consent. The places where the wound had healed became tougher; they hardened like the bones of young children and resisted the least alteration with fierce pain.

The whistlers sat, during this procedure, three in a row on a long bench, wrapped in white sheets up to the chin, as though they were going to be shaved. They held the long bent tube whose end projected from the mouth firmly in one hand, for owing to its smooth surface and the wild convulsions into which the gullet was thrown by the effort to get rid of it, it was impossible to hold it with the teeth alone. With the other hand they drummed on their knees, at the same time passing the third finger without ceasing over the thumb. For it was a positive longing to give vent to their pain in some way or another; sometimes, too, they stamped violently with their feet. But the longer they kept the tube in the gullet, the longer there was for their endurance to assert its influence and to accustom the tissues more radically to the new condition. So the doctor said, and so, too, the nurses; nor were the whistlers behindhand, till at last from pride they prolonged the healing torture of their own free will. One morning, while she stood at the disposal of the doctor when he was putting in the tubes, the theatre sister said that they were curious to see which of the whistlers was the bravest and could hold out the longest. Now the word "brave" in reality meant singularly little to the whistlers. It went without saying, or at any rate they had had enough of it. Nevertheless, from then onwards, they sat side by side without a movement, merely groaning softly, and with stolen glances measured themselves against each other, till their hands trembled and the sweat trickled in streams down their foreheads. Then Pointner and Benjamin usually snatched their tubes out at the same moment, while Kollin sat on a moment longer though he allowed not a sign of triumph to escape him. Nevertheless, Pointner sometimes showed his annoyance. He tapped his forehead lightly in disdain and rolled his eyes upwards—a favourite gesture of his. The next day, however, he would pit all his strength to come off the victor.

For the whistlers were devoted to their doctor with all their hearts, and held him in secret wonder and veneration, although they never spoke of him among themselves except with the kind of tolerance extended to a chum, and made no end of fun over many of his peculiarities. Although he could not be more than a few years older than Pointner and Kollin, they always called him the "old 'un," and when he joked with them in his jolly and at the same time merciless way, or even praised them for their pluck, they smiled and cast down their eyes and were so overcome with pride that they did not know what to say. Then, as soon as ever he was out of the room, replies of the utmost wit and familiarity occurred to them, and they bragged before the others of all they might so easily have said.

The "old 'un," Doctor Quint, as his name really was, always came in in a blinding white medical overall which gave off an odour of powerful disinfectants and strong vinegar; beneath it were to be seen the creased trousers of an English suit. He wore bright silk socks and shining patent leather shoes. He liked bright red ties, and preferred that colour to any other because, as he said, it was a red rag to all priests. Owing to a certain refractory attitude that he had in official matters and his unconcealed contempt for the military hierarchy, he was not in the good books of the superior officers in control of the clinic; but as he was exceptionally gifted and spent all his great energy to the point of exhaustion in the service of sick and wounded, nothing further had come of several very carefully formulated reports in his disfavour. He had a small white face, very broad shoulders and well-knit frame, and all the sisters and nurses blushed when he went along the corridors with quick elastic steps, with his hands sunk in the pockets of his overall. His eyes were large and dark and fiery; but they were set at an angle to each other and for this reason it was his habit to conceal one of them with the concave ophthalmoscope which he used in his examinations. He was seldom seen without it in any part of the clinic. It was very much of the shape and circumference of a small saucer, and was kept in position by a leather band round the forehead. In the middle of it, just large enough to spy through, was a small aperture which had, as well, the effect of concentrating the light. When he sat in front of a wounded man with this instrument, it seemed that while his spy-glass eye was busied in scrutiny and diagnosis, the other roved sideways into the distance, as though he were already meditating new methods of healing; and this the whistlers firmly believed to be the case. For this reason as though by tacit agreement they never made fun over his eyes, and it was their dearest wish to look one day through this spy-glass with the light directed into it. What they expected from this great moment knew no bounds.

Doctor Quint had the strength of a giant. To keep himself fit it was his practice to wrestle with enormous weights and lift them on high, and to make a sport of handling great iron bowls and disks of a terrifying circumference. He took a pleasure in displaying these feats of strength to the whistlers before operating on them. While the nurses were still busy strapping Kollin on to the operating table, he suddenly grasped the heavy iron surgical chair that stood in the same room and held it up in his outstretched arm.

"Do that, Pioneer," he said impressively after a moment, looking down upon him over his shoulders. Kollin, who had just been made fast with the knee-strap, smiled with astonishment. Even though he was not at the moment in a position to take up the challenge, yet the invitation to do so cheered him to the utmost, and he made up his mind to attempt it with another chair as a preliminary as soon as ever he had the opportunity. After that he submitted himself quietly to the knife with boundless confidence.

The compass of Doctor Quint's voice answered to these exhibitions of strength. As a rule he did not speak unusually loud, but occasionally it amused him to throw the nurses into alarm and consternation by suddenly giving vent to a sort of trumpeting over his work. Often while they were still sitting over their breakfast in their room the whistlers heard him in the far distant treatment rooms shouting at the top of his voice for an injection-needle or a basin. Then they raised their heads and listened with delight and nodded knowingly to each other. As a rule Doctor Quint appeared not long after in the passage outside the door, winking out of the corners of his eyes and strolling along with a man, who had just been operated on, resting like a doll on his arms, while the nurses, half pleased and half upset, wheeled the stretcher along in his rear. He chose the heaviest and stoutest among all the lot of wounded for this manœuvre, and then laid them carefully in their beds wrapped in their blankets and still in the deep sleep of the anæsthetic.

Nevertheless, he hated any shouting on the part of others. There was not the least occasion for whimpering and shouting, he informed his patients before a painful operation without an anæsthetic. He begged them to forbear, with the assurance that taken as a whole the affair would be perfectly painless. He granted that one bad moment could not be avoided. Of this he would give warning and then they might roar. As a rule after this the victims sat quietly without making a sound, till he suddenly threw knife and forceps into the basin, pulled the spy-glass out of his eye, and, with a look over his shoulders at the next man, announced that it was over. But not everyone was altogether satisfied. For many had been waiting for the promised moment when they might emit the terrific howl that they had been storing up.

But to the whistlers he said: "Shout, Pointner! Shout, Bombardier!" and, holding them round the shoulders in a tight embrace, pressed down the agonising rod with relentless force past the scars in their throats: and they loved him for it.

VII

ONE morning, not long after his arrival, Benjamin went for a walk through the halls and corridors of the hospital. At that time he was still quite voiceless. He wished to visit a comrade with whom he had been at school. On his way he mistook the door and found himself in the ward of the blind. They sat in a green half-light on their beds or on chairs, many with bandages as in blind man's buff, and all with faces slightly raised in the always-listening attitude peculiar to them.

"Well, comrade, who are you? and what have you got?" Sergeant Wichtermann said after a moment, from a wheeled chair by a window. Sergeant Wichtermann had got the whole burst of a bomb in front of Arras. Nevertheless he was not killed, for, as he said, he had a strong constitution. But he was blind and had not a limb left but one arm with two fingers, and in these two he held a long pipe.

Benjamin was very much frightened. He drummed at once with his hand on the door behind him, so as at least to give a token of his presence; and at the same time he looked anxiously round, in the hope of discovering a man with one eye who would be able to explain why he preserved so unfitting a silence in the ward of the blind. But there was not one to be seen.

"Well," Wichtermann growled, "can't you open your mouth? Are you making fools of us?" "I'll soon put him in tune," promised another, getting down from his bed in a rage and showing his fists. A well-aimed slipper came hurtling through the air and struck the door close behind Benjamin's head. Benjamin delayed his departure no longer.

By good fortune he found Landwerhmann Ferge, whom he knew already, just outside the door. Ferge was a good-natured Thuringian with a pasty-coloured moustache on his sallow face, but he was not well received among his fellows. It must be explained that he bore an evil nickname. A bullet had gone right through his seat and torn the bowel. In order to give this very susceptible organ time to heal the doctors had made for him another temporary orifice in the region of his hip, and this unfortunately was always open. For this reason Ferge was forced to wear on his naked skin under his shirt a large india-rubber bag. This condemned him to a lonely existence and doubled and tripled the bitterness of his peculiar plight. For Ferge all his life long had had a passion for card play—that is for watching others play with an interest all the keener because his stinginess prevented him taking a hand himself. In earlier days this had been his favourite Sunday pastime; and now he might have whiled away entire months in the indulgence of this passion. For everywhere indoors and out in the garden, the halt and the maimed sat in three and fours and played sheepshead, skat and doublehead, and on still days there was a murmur and thunder, gentle and fascinating, from behind every door, of the trumps that were there slapped down upon the tables. But his comrades drove him off because of his smell, and so he wandered about in the park in the open air, longing for the day when his shame and torment would be removed from him.

Hence he was now cheered to the heart when at last someone had need of him. He took Benjamin back among the blind and explained to them in a short address how it came that he had been dumb. The blind were immediately reconciled. They came round him eagerly, and each in turn touched his silver mouthpiece and held their hands in front of the warm stream of air that issued from it. Even Sergeant Wichtermann had himself wheeled up in his chair, and with his two fingers made a precise investigation of the tube, saying all the while: "I understand, I understand."

"The doctors make all you want," he said at length very jovially. "One gets a new mouth and another a new backside. But after all it's not the right one, except that you're more easily known by it, Comrade Ferge." At that everyone laughed uproariously. But Ferge sadly and silently withdrew and took his evil smell with him.

After this the whistlers often visited the blind to play draughts or chess with them. For this the blind had chessmen half of whom were furnished with little round tops of lead. Also they were not simply placed on the board, but fixed in it with little pegs so that the groping fingers should not upset them. On these occasions Deuster, an army medical corporal, always greeted the whistlers with a finished imitation of their croaking manner of speech, to the delight of all, the whistlers included. Deuster was very small and red haired. His face and hands were thickly covered with freckles. He had lost his sight while bringing in one of the enemy who lay wounded on the wire in front of the trench. The cries of this man were so lamentable that they got on everybody's nerves in the trench and set them jangling, till at last, as Deuster said, it was more than a man could bear any longer.

Pointner was particularly fond of him and was always as pleased to see him as if he were a new discovery, for he was the only one among the blind who was now and then to be beaten at draughts or chess. For they saw everything as they had it in their own minds, and the opponent had scarcely made his move before their hands flitted over the board to ascertain his intentions and then replied at once in accordance with the well thought-out plan to which they clung meanwhile in their darkness with undeviating purpose. Deuster alone, who loved to chatter, sometimes made gross blunders, whereat Pointner was so beside himself for joy and delight that he jumped up and, skipping behind his chair, threw his arms affectionately round the neck of his conquered opponent. "Blind man of Hess," he said to him, and admonished him like a father to keep his eyes in his fingers next time.

For it was the custom in the hospital for the patients to chaff each other over their infirmities; they found a certain consolation in it. Fusileer Kulka for example, from what was then the province of Posen, who for a time occupied the spare bed in the whistlers' room, rarely spoke to them without pressing his finger to an imaginary tube and rattling in his throat. He could only speak broken German, but he delighted in recounting in his singsong voice how he came to lose his leg. He was lying in the open with his company after it had swarmed out in an engagement with Siberian infantry, when a bullet ripped his left cheek and passed out through his ear. At that Fusileer Kulka unstrapped his pack and got out a little mirror that he kept in it. He just wanted to see how he looked, for he had a bride at home. While taking a leisurely survey he must have exposed himself too far, for a machine gunner got his range and shot him twelve times in the left leg. Now he he had one of leather and steel.

The whistlers took him between them when he practised walking with it outside their room. Kollin on his right, Benjamin on his left, they tottered with earnest demeanour up and down the corridor. The whistlers, too, now appeared to have false legs. Just as Kulka did, they hoisted one shoulder and hip to the fore at every step, at the same time sinking a little on one side. When it came to turning about however, Benjamin, for preference, got into great difficulties. He hopped helplessly on one leg where he stood and tried in vain to steady himself with the false one. Finally he fell at full length, and then, raising his stick, he began to chastise the refractory leg with it. At that Fusileer Kulka laughed so immeasurably that the tears ran down his cheeks and he threatened to fall over backwards in earnest. This happened outside the door of the blind, and instantly the army medical corporal, Deuster, came groping his way out and desired to know what the joke might be, for he was always eager to join in a laugh and for ever on the look out for an opportunity.

On a later occasion he went for a walk with Benjamin in the park. Some days before he had been with the rest to a fine concert. Never in his life, he confessed, had he ever known anything so beautiful. From that day he had made up his mind to become a musician as soon as he was released from hospital, though he could not play any instrument and would first have to learn. He had been a worker in a cloth factory.

"Comrade," he said in an ecstasy, standing still after he had exposed his project, "it comes from within. It is all inside one. He who has it in him, can—" Suddenly he stopped as though he no longer knew what he had been going to say, or had himself abruptly lost belief in it. He lifted his face and fixed it on Benjamin's. He blinked his hollow eyes without ceasing, and the corners of his mouth began to twitch. But Benjamin knew no more than he what to say. So he took him by the arm and led him, now dumb, back to the room of the blind.

VIII

FUSILEER KULKA had been released and sent home and the year had once more passed into summer, when one morning the volunteer Jäger, Fürlein' made his appearance in the whistlers' room. Still clothed in his green uniform just as he had been sent to them by Doctor Quint, he stood among the whistlers and laboriously expounded to them what the situation was in which he found himself. He had not been wounded, but, from a cause that so far could not be explained, had suddenly lost his voice and it was an effort for him to produce even a hoarse whisper. At dawn, after a night under canvas, he had just crept out of his tent to pass on an order—and then he found this change in himself, and even with the air, as he said, he had had difficulty from then onwards. Even now he could sometimes scarcely breathe, and on such occasions an anxious expression came over his face and he hastily removed the clumsy shooting spectacles from his nose as though this would bring him relief.

The faces of the whistlers, however, cleared at once. With cheering and consoling nods, as though they knew all about it long ago and were in secret possession of chosen remedies for this very case, they corroborated all that he could say; and Pointner with long deliberation felt his lean neck with his supple fingers, while with a collected expression he stared past him into a corner. Fürlein, meanwhile, glanced shyly at the white bibs that surrounded him—from beneath which a slender cheeping and rustling sounded from time to time. Finally they all clapped him on the shoulder and told him to cheer up. "The old 'un will soon see to it," they said, and looked meaningly at one another. Then they conducted him to his bed, and Kollin went hastily to the cupboard and returned with one of the striped linen garments such as they all wore.

Fürlein's condition seemed to grow worse during the next days; more and more frequently he had to struggle with slight attacks of suffocation, and sometimes even swallowing gave him trouble. But Doctor Quint did nothing with him for the time. He was going to wait a bit longer, he said, with an impenetrable expression. The whistlers, however, had already decided that Fürlein was destined to be one of them. Kollin, on the very first day, had suggested to the theatre-sister, whom he helped in cleaning the instruments, that she should see to it, and quickly, that the Jäger got his tube, and she had declined abruptly to have anything to do with it. Now they tried Fürlein. The three of them gathered in the evening at his bedside and began talking to him intimately, kindly and also a little patronisingly. It was as though they had a rare favour to bestow. Fürlein, who had been in secret fear of something like this, plaintively shook his head.

Gradually, however, the whistlers, who had set their hearts on it, won on his confidence, though at the cost of indefatigable efforts, and persuaded him to look at their tubes with a mixture of curiosity and aversion. He was still heartily afraid of the operation, but at the same time he began to put his trust in it, and his impatience became more and more apparent. After it was over he would soon be quite at his ease. He actually looked forward to the time, he assured them with a helpless smile. The whistlers enthusiastically concurred. Did they not breathe more freely and easily than ever, perhaps, in their lives? No one could have any notion who was not himself a whistler. Kollin raised his bib, drew a deep breath and exhaled it again with a triumphant air, while he fanned to and fro with his hand in front of the little opening. Benjamin, for his part, did not know how to say enough for the undisturbed sleep he could enjoy at any hour. As a prompt demonstration he got into bed in his clothes and covered himself over up to his neck. He put the large pillow over his face till nothing was to be seen of him. But through a little gap between the bed clothes and the pillow he breathed in at his tube, and Fürlein looked with all his eyes at this marvellous phenomenon that had so uncanny a fascination for him.

His days were happy now. He began to learn, as they called it, and drew out the inner tubes from the whistlers' necks and cleaned them. Or he cut out new bibs for them and neatly pinned them on. And the whistlers made him returns. He was permitted to be the first to read the paper; many a choice morsel to which the kitchen maids gave them a secret priority was allotted him, and they poured him out a double allowance of the beer or wine which occasionally found its way to their room by the channel of private munificence.

At length early one summer morning, before seven o'clock, Fürlein was sent for to the operating theatre, and the whistlers, much elated, conducted him a part of the way. But against all expectation, he came back after a quarter of an hour while they were still busily employed making his bed ready and putting the blocks under its feet at the lower end; for those who were operated upon in the neck had at first to lie with their heads lower than their feet, in case the blood ran into the ramifications of the windpipe. Fürlein came back, not on the wheeled stretcher, but on his feet as he had gone, and he had not, either, any bandage on his neck. Doctor Quint had sent a strong electric current through his throat and suddenly ordered him to shout. Immediately Jäger Fürlein uttered a loud shout, and now he could speak and breathe again as of old. He explained all this to the whistlers with downcast eyes, and they heard him without making a sound. He had a fine rousing voice. So much it was easy to hear though he took great pains to damp it down.

"It's all for the best, comrade," said Fürlein at last to each one of the circle round him, and held out his hand. The whistlers slowly recovered themselves and with forced smiles offered their congratulations. After that they betook themselves all three to the park for their rest in the open air; Fürlein in any case could not accompany them, for he was to be sent at once to his unit at the base and had to pack up his effects. Also he had the pretext of having his papers put in order. When they came in again at mid-day, the Jäger was no longer there. He had gone without saying good-bye, and the whistlers readily understood. But they never spoke of him any more.

I X

IN the third autumn of the war, however, a fourth comrade was added to the whistlers in earnest. One afternoon Sister Emily, a red-cheeked Valkyrie of uncertain age, came in and laid a heap of clean clothes on the fourth bed that since Fürlein's departure had stood unmade up in the corner.

"Early to-morrow there's a new whistler coming, and a real one this time," she said in her robust tones, as she turned down the sheet over the heavy blanket, "and what d'you think—it's an English prisoner."

The whistlers pricked up their ears and shook their heads. Pointner noisily pushed back his chair and laid down his spoon. "No," he said loudly, and the other two showed their indignation in their faces.

"It's not a bit of use," said Sister Emily emphatically, and shook up the pillow. "He has been shot through the throat like you, and there's nowhere else for him to go for treatment. So you must just put up with him."

Herewith she pulled a piece of chalk out of the pocket of her apron and wrote on the nameplate at the head of the empty bed. "Harry Flint" was now to be read there;

and below, where in other cases a man's rank was stated— "Englishman." Pointner still signified his distaste with one or two gestures of his hands, and brought the coffee jug threateningly down on the table. Then he rammed his cap down on one side and went out into the garden, spitting with rage like a cat.

The next morning when the whistlers were sitting over their breakfast, the door slowly opened and there entered a round-faced boy with large brown eyes and thick blue-black hair. In his hand he held a small bundle about the size of a head of cabbage. He wore the hospital uniform of blue and white striped linen, and over it a kind of round cape. On his head was an utterly washed-out cap of the same material and far too small for him. It was Harry Flint, in German Heini Kieselstein, or simply Kiesel, of the Gloucesters. He stood blushing in the doorway, and, putting his hand to his cap by way of greeting, made at the same time something like a slight bow. After that he remained fixed in an appealing attitude, his hands laid one over the other at the level of his waist, and looked steadily at the three whistlers with a mixture of shame, pride and fear.

The whistlers did not appear to see him. Each looked straight in front of him over his cup, and so contrived to avoid the eyes of the others. After a while Harry once more saluted, and his eyes began to fill with tears. Pointner sat mouthing a large piece of soaked bread with a long knife in his hand, and at this he jerked the knife over his shoulder in the direction of the vacant bed. Harry Flint betook himself there at once and sat down gingerly on the edge of it, as though he desired to show that he made the least possible claim on the air space of the room. Directly afterwards the whistlers got up all together for a walk in the garden, and left the rifleman to himself without deigning to cast him a glance.

When they came back again at mid-day they found Harry sweeping out the room with a broom and shovel that he had found for himself. It was now apparent that he wore his tube in his neck without any protective covering and secured only by a thin cord. It looked as though he had a large metal button or a screw stuck in the front of his throat. Kollin shook his head and went up to him, and, leading him by the sleeve to the cupboard at his bedside, took a clean piece of muslin out of the drawer and pinned it carefully and neatly under his chin. Harry, who had stood without a movement, took a small looking-glass from his pocket and looked at himself with delight. Then he rummaged in his bundle and produced a stick of chocolate and offered it to Kollin. Kollin gave it a passing glance and quietly shook his head. Harry bit his lip and turned away.

At this time food was scarce in Germany, and white bread, cake, meat and imported fruit had vanished. Harry, however, had no lack of them. Soon after his arrival a large parcel of otherwise unprocurable food came for him from an English Prisoners of War Committee in Switzerland, and regularly every third and fourth day came another. Harry handed it all round in the friendliest way—smoked bacon, wurst in cans, butter in tin tubes, biscuits with nuts and almonds, and white bread with brown and shining crust. But though the whistlers had long forgotten their hatred of Great Britain, they obstinately refused to touch even a morsel of it.

It was not always their loss. For sometimes the parcels were a long time on the road, and then there was a dangerous hissing and effervescing when Harry stuck in the tin-opener. The meat smelled like bad cheese, and the bread was not to be cut with any knife. This put the whistlers in the best of moods. They surrounded the table on which Harry had spread his treasures, and in the mixture of German and English that had become meanwhile the common whistler lingo, passed the severest criticisms on England and English products. "What muck!" they croaked, and showed their disgust by holding their noses. This was always a disconcerting moment for Harry. He could not admit that Britain presented a Briton with bad fare. With indignant eyes he soaked his bread in his soup and rubbed salt in the putrid meat. And then he swallowed it all down, and patting his stomach endeavoured to show by his face how much he enjoyed it. Often, however, he turned pale and hurried out and vomited long and painfully for the honour of Great Britain.

The originator of the common German-English whistler-language was Benjamin. After he had overcome his first modesty he brought forward his grammar-school English and initiated Harry into the usages and rules of the hospital, and in particular of the whistlers' room. He instructed him also in the art of speaking, or rather croaking, by stopping the mouth of the tube with the finger-tip, and began to teach him a little German. Harry was a quick pupil, and soon transformed himself from the dumb and constrained foreigner into a friend who was always ready for a talk. The whistlers got to be very fond of him.

One day he confided to Benjamin that he was married. A war-marriage, he called it. He was twenty and Mrs. Flint of Gloucester a little over sixteen. Benjamin had often found him seated on his bed in the act, apparently, of smelling, or indeed tasting, a sheet of note paper, and had been at a loss for the explanation. And now Harry revealed it. Mrs. Flint was allowed by the censorship to send no more than four sides of note paper to her prisoner husband every week. But writing was no easy task for her; she had, as Harry confessed, first to set about learning how to do it. For this reason each letter contained no more than one or two laboured sentences, traced in large letters on lines previously ruled out. The remaining space, three and a half sides, was covered with small neatly formed crosses. Each one of them, Harry explained, betokened a kiss of wedded love. Harry loyally responded to each. Even in the darkness of the night his lips often met those of his far-distant wife on the paper. Benjamin, whose bed was opposite his, could hear the rustling folds and the sighs of the prisoner. Once he got up and groped his way across to console him with a joke. But Harry quickly pulled the bedclothes over his head because his face was wet with tears.

X

NOT long after, as winter drew on, Pointner became bedridden. His heart began to feel the strain of the poison that circled in his veins. Yet he was very happy at that time. He lay quietly and without pain in bed and read until far into the night. True, he was soon at an end with the love and murder stories in the library, but, to make up, a thick volume containing the complete fairy tales of the brothers Grimm, that Benjamin had taken out one day, became his inseparable companion. Over and over again he read with a blissful smile the stories of Fitcher's bird, of Jorinda and Joringel, of Rapunzel, of the Blue Light, and the old man made young again, although he knew them now by heart; and Benjamin marvelled over him, while Kollin sadly shook his head. Sometimes he laughed silently to himself and laid the book for a while in his lap, but not for a moment letting it out of his hands; or he beckoned Benjamin to him and laying his finger on the title of the story handed him the book without a word. Lying quietly on his side he watched his expression closely, and when

Benjamin smiled his whole face lit up; then he sat up and croaked:

> "*Als hinaus*
> *Nach des Herrn Korbes seimem Haus.*"

or

> "*Sind wir nicht Knaben glatt und fein,*
>   *Was wollen wir länger Schuster sein?*"*

then lay back again, waved his head to and fro and shook with laughter.

Often when the other two had gone for a walk, Harry Flint sat for hours together by his bed and took care of him. He cleaned his tube, put him a clean bib under his chin, gave him a drink, and pulled his bed clothes straight; or else he just sat still and communicated something of his own vitality by his mere presence. It got so far that Pointner did not even persist in refusing the cakes of white flour from Great Britain. Harry soaked them in milk and gave them to him in a spoon.

It happened thus. One morning there had been an unexpected inspection of the drawers of the bedside cupboards, and in each one the Sister found a broken packet of beautiful English short-bread. She took a piece of

---

* "We are going to the house of Herr Korbes"

"Now we are boys so fine to see,

Why should we longer cobblers be?"

These are lines from two of Grimm's fairytales, *Herr Korbes* (Mr Korbes) and *Die Wichtelmänner* (The Elves) respectively.

it and exclaimed how good it was. But the whistlers went very red, and Harry Flint went reddest of all and hastily left the room: for he had gone by night to each one's bed, to-day to Benjamin's, to-morrow to Kollin's, and last to Pointner's, and given a packet to each of them in turn. Thereupon the whistlers could hold out no longer, and also each thought he was the only one who secretly beneath his bed clothes nibbled at the honour of the Fatherland. From that morning they assisted Harry without any disguise to demolish the white bread and the admirable wurst. It benefited Harry too, for he could now confess it openly when the bacon was bad or the butter rancid, and was no longer under the necessity of making himself ill.

One day, when the two were alone together, Pointner took his English cap out of its hiding place and put it on Harry's head. Harry stood motionless with head erect and beamed with delight. It was his dearest wish to possess this cap. Among the various buildings of the hospital, which in peace time was a State clinic, there were some devoted to patients from the civil population. They wore the same patient's uniform as the soldiers but for the military caps, and this distinction was so punctiliously preserved that a soldier-patient was seldom seen without his cap. When occasion demanded they had them on their heads even in bed. Harry, too, was a soldier, but he was no longer in possession of an English cap, and as he could not wear a German one, he was compelled to go about bareheaded, or else in that little boy's cap of linen, and to let himself be taken for a civilian patient. He suffered the more because nearly all the civilians of his age and height were at that time in the skin clinic, which was called the Ritterburg and given as wide a berth as possible.

Even the soldiers who had to have temporary quarters there, were left during that time to themselves. Moreover it was there that the so-called *Ritter-fräulein*—women of ill-fame from the town—were subjected to compulsory cure. They were not permitted to leave the floor assigned to them except on rare occasions; though it was said that they swung their cavaliers up to their rooms at night by means of ropes of twisted sheets. However the rest might enjoy these tales and find in them an inexhaustible topic of conversation, not one of them would have anything to do with the building or its occupants, let alone being mistaken for one of them.

The trouble was that Pointner could not bring himself to part with his trophy. But he allowed Harry to wear it now and then when no one was about. There was nothing then that Harry more eagerly desired than to be taken by surprise with the cap on his head. But no sooner was a step heard outside, than Pointner whipped it away and hid it under the clothes. He promised him, however, that he would leave him the cap at his death. He gave Harry his hand on it, and Harry grasped it in token of acceptance and stood to attention with a solemn and ceremonial air. It was soon to come true.

X I

BEFORE that, however, Benjamin himself had to go to the Ritterburg. One day, to his horror, he discovered inexplicable and painful symptoms on his body. But from shame he could not confide to anybody the state he was in; he kept silence in the desperate hope that the malady would pass over of itself, and that one morning he would wake up healed and cleansed as though it had all been a dream. But the pain only got worse and loathsome spots began to spread all over his body. At last there was nothing for it but to tell Herr Mauch all about it—perhaps he would be able to help him without Doctor Quint and the Sister needing to know anything of it.

Herr Mauch, as he was called, a greyhaired and moustachio'd Landsturm man, was the orderly of the department. It was his duty to perform the heavier bodily labours. He stood by when patients were moved from one bed to another, or bathed. He washed the dead and conveyed them into the cellar, where a postmortem was sometimes carried out. Also he went to and fro with the commode when required, and had charge of the various vessels that ministered to necessities. He was the first

PAUL ALVERDES

to appear every morning, making a jovial entry to each room with a clinking wire basket in which he collected the glass bottles, making very knowing comments the while. He wore a peakless service cap with the Landwehr cross on the badge, and an old pair of service trousers, also the regulation canvas tunic and a large apron. He laid great stress on being a military personage, although the source of his never-failing good spirits was in having, as he said, got hold of a fine job that protected him from being called up and sent to the front. For this reason he carried out every part of his duties with the utmost preciseness.

He was none the less frank in his admiration of his wounded companions-in-arms, and loved to address them as "old soldier" or even as "corporal." There was nothing he delighted in more than the most bloodthirsty adventures from the battles on all fronts; and these alone could sometimes delay him on his round with the bottle-basket. For a wounded soldier was often disposed for a talk at early dawn, and then he would set down his receptacle for a moment and spur the narrator on with enthusiastic exclamations and encouraging questions as to the fierce slaughter of one enemy after another. "On, on to battle! For battle are we born! for battle are we ready!" he hummed with a defiant look while he collected the rest of the bottles and betook himself to the next room. The few civilian patients, on the other hand, who now and then came under his care, he treated with scorn. "For you," he used to say when one of them addressed him as Mauch, "for a shirker like you, I am Herr Mauch!" Hence the soldiers, too, always called him Herr Mauch, though they addressed him familiarly with "thou."

His usual haunt was the bath-house of the hospital. Here he looked after all his various utensils in a bustle of soda and soapsuds, cleaned boots, made sundry lists and held himself in readiness in case he was needed. For the most part he sat upon his perambulatory chair with an air cushion for upholstery on its lid. Here he carried on a secret traffic in supernumerary bottles of beer, as he called them, from the hospital stores, for he stole like a crow. On occasion a leave certificate was to be had through him, and indeed all kinds of bartering transacted.

"God damn me!" said Herr Mauch with jovial astonishment when Benjamin with trembling hands had undone his clothes. Then he put down his cup. "God damn me, Corporal, you've got the Turkish music." By this was to be understood the severest form of venereal disease. "How on earth did you get that?"

Benjamin knew no more than he did. He had never been with a woman in his life. "Help me, Herr Mauch," he brought out in a voice that almost failed him, and almost fell backwards over the edge of the bath he was sitting on. But Herr Mauch could do nothing of the sort. No, he couldn't help him there, he said. It must be reported to Doctor Quint, otherwise it would end in the other fellows getting it too.

Benjamin staggered out. As he knew of no other place where he could be undisturbed, he shut himself in a closet and stood squeezed in a corner with dry eyes, while his teeth chattered and shudders shook his whole frame. Whatever else had happened in him and around him had been within his comprehension and he had accepted it. But now he had come to the end. So he resolved to die.

When he had actually pulled out the tube from his neck, so that the little opening in which it was placed might speedily close up, he was aware of a soft chirping sound above him, and looking up over the top of the partition wall that separated the one compartment from the next, he saw the anxious face of Harry Flint of Gloucester. A moment later the door was forced and Herr Mauch rushed in with a loud cry and hauled him out. Harry had seen Benjamin vanish, and noticed his tottering steps and distraught expression; and when Benjamin did not return within a reasonable time, he stole softly into the neighbouring compartment, climbed upon the window ledge, and from there looked down over the partition.

Doctor Quint, to whom Herr Mauch had meanwhile reported the matter, was even paler than usual. The first thing he did was to take hold of the halfunconscious Benjamin and insert a new tube with considerable force through the opening which was indeed already closing up. Then he pulled the spy-glass from his forehead and examined Benjamin's spots through a powerful microscope, and at once his face became more and more serene. "Scabies," he then said quietly. "Prurigo, a perfectly normal prurigo, my boy. You must go straight across to the Ritterburg. In three days you'll be clean again."

Tears fell fast down Benjamin's cheeks. His chin worked convulsively to and fro; he was shaken with violent sobs and he laughed for joy. Doctor Quint turned about on his revolving stool. "Idiot!" he bellowed in a terrible voice. "Blockhead! Child-murderer! I'll have you court-martialled and shot." But Herr Mauch had already bolted through the door.

Thus it was that Benjamn got to the Ritterburg without being allowed, owing to the risk of infection, to return to his comrades first.

There an experienced hand smeared him at once from head to foot with a corrosive ointment of a greenish colour. The shirt, too, that was given him to put on was green, and the cotton gloves as well. Even the beds were green from the ointment, and the very wall paper of the room into which he was taken. For this reason it was called the hunters' room and its occupants the hunters. There were half a dozen of them there together.

The oldest of them was a white-haired tramp who hated doctors. His bed was next to Benjamin's. "They're liars," he informed him, and gratefully ate Benjamin's rations, for Benjamin ate nothing the whole time he had to stay in the hunters' room. "It is all rubbish they tell us about the little animals. It is in the blood, deep in the blood, and it comes out as the trees come out. For why should I get it otherwise every spring? But sometimes it stays till the autumn. Then it is against nature and something has to be done to check it."

Benjamin scarcely listened to him. He looked down through the window into the yellowing garden of the

Ritterburg. It was strictly shut off from the park, where anybody could walk about. There in the midst of a bevy of Ritterburg *fräulein* was a yellow-skinned fellow with black hair gleaming in the pale mid-day sunlight. He was called the Legionary, for he was a deserter from the Foreign Legion, who had got back through the lines to Germany. He had a wild face, beautiful and adventurous, and Benjamin began to lose himself in dreams of the amazing experiences that he seemed to be telling the girls around him.

XII

NOT long after Benjamin's return to the whistlers' room, Doctor Quint carried out on him and Harry what he hoped would prove the final and decisive operation, and they had to lie in bed in great pain and with high fever. Kollin, the only one now left on his legs, entered on dreary days. Since Benjamin's arrival, card games had taken their place beside the ever-beloved chess in the daily life of the whistlers, games that three or four could play. The excitement and the scoring they involved, and also the passionate discussion after the game was over, as to how everything had had to be, or might have been if this trump had been held back or that trick had been taken, had all been for Kollin the keenest joy. It carried him past his disappointment at being always a loser at cards, for he played a clever and cunning game, but in this as in all else he had no luck.

Now, however, the luck suddenly turned in his favour. Sitting alone at the table he shuffled and dealt to himself and two imaginary partners with the most exact precision. Then he turned his hand up and, sure enough, he had the game all in his hands, untakable solos and grands with all the aces and knaves as well. Time after time he jumped up, with the cards spread in his hand, and hurried over to Pointner's and Benjamin's beds to show them the incontestable assurance of victory and luck. Pointner, who had suddenly begun to sink and could seldom now read his fairy tales, only waved a hand feebly and turned away, and Benjamin looked at him through a daze of narcotics with fevered, gleaming eyes, but did not know him. At last Kollin reported to Doctor Quint and begged him to do with him as with the two others, for they were his comrades. But Doctor Quint could not risk it yet in his case, and had to console him by holding out hopes for the future.

Thus passed monotonous days. Outside it snowed on and on, and sometimes a regimental band took up its position before the windows on a patch from which the snow had been shovelled, and played the usual rousing tunes. Harry Flint always showed the liveliest pleasure when at the close "Hail to thee in conqueror's wreath" was played, for it had the same tune as the hymn in which God is prayed to save the gracious King of Great Britain. He sat up in bed, and, putting on a ceremonial and dignified expression, beat time with his finger.

Sometimes Sergeant Wichtermann had himself wheeled in on his chair and discussed the military situation with Kollin. He was very confident and prognosticated a speedy victory. He would then contemplate taking part in his regiment's triumphal return from a carriage. Harry, meanwhile, pricked up his ears and sadly shook his head, but Kollin, too, who sat carving a set of chessmen that he intended as a present to Pointner, looked grave. He got up and took from his drawer a paper on which he had worked out in figures a statement of all the allied and enemy forces. He began to read it carefully through while he followed the rows of figures with his finger. There, for him, lay the answer to this question.

Harry and Benjamin had not been long on their feet again, with the hope that they might soon be quit of their tubes, when Pointner's end came. Often he lay unconscious and slowly, without ceasing, turned his head this way and that, as though he were always wondering about something. His face had become small and peaceful like the face of a child, and his eyes, when he opened them, were always a deeper and deeper blue. But he opened them seldom now, and when he did the other whistlers collected at once round his bed and joked with him and he smiled and looked tenderly at them.

One morning early, when they were all still in bed, they heard him getting restless. He was rattling violently at the cupboard by his bed, and a glass fell with a crash to the floor. They made a light, and there sat Pointner upright in bed holding out the English cap to Harry. Harry jumped up and ran across in bare feet to prop him up; but Pointner had already sunk slowly back. His eyes were fixed on the ceiling, and he did not move again.

He was buried in the little soldiers' cemetery behind the park. In the first row behind the coffin walked the three whistlers, for even Harry Flint, by the special intercession of

Doctor Quint, was permitted, as an exception (so they called it), to go too. He wore for the first time the English cap.

Immediately behind them walked Herr Mauch. He had girded on a bayonet, and also procured himself a helmet which, being too big for him, fell sideways on his head at every step. On his arm he had the army medical corporal, Deuster, beside whom went Backhuhn, whose nose was now very nearly completed. The band played the Comrades' Song, and Herr Mauch sobbed aloud into his helmet which he held before his moustache. Benjamin and Harry Flint were shaking too and looked with drawn faces to the ground. Kollin alone kept a calm face and dry eyes, but when his turn came to step in front of the heap of earth and scatter some of it into the grave, he put the spade aside and threw on to the coffin the chessmen that he had brought with him in his overcoat pocket.

A few weeks later he was wheeled into the operating theatre on a stretcher; for the final critical operation was now to be put to the test in his case too. But Benjamin and Harry waited in vain for his return. When they saw him again he was dead behind the white folding screen in Herr Mauch's bath-house, where, when there was time, it was the practice to convey the dying: for it had been found that the sight of a dying man often had a dangerous influence on the others and drew them in his train.

And then the day came when Doctor Quint drew the silver pipes from the necks of the two survivors. The little mouth above the breast closed in one night and they could now breathe almost like other people.

"No longer whistlers," Harry whispered. But they did not venture to show their joy. Arm in arm they walked along the garden paths and drew deep breaths.

One morning, when they were both lying on their beds in their clothes and sleeping, Herr Mauch came in with a sheaf of papers under his arm. "Get up, Harry Flint," he called. "Get ready sharp. You've been exchanged and are going home. You must be dressed in half an hour. There's still time to catch a train to-day to Rotterdam." Therewith he threw a bundle of clothes on the bed. Harry slowly sat up and stared across in consternation at Benjamin. "No," he said. "No. Not going away. Staying here." Only by degrees he began to understand. Slowly a gleam lit up in his eyes, and do as he might he could not hide it. With trembling hands he pulled off his hospital uniform and put on the khaki one. It came from the disinfecting room and was faded and little but rags.

Then he sat down on his bed with his hands laid one on the other, and his bundle at his feet, just as he had sat the first time on the day of his arrival. Again and again he looked at Benjamin and Benjamin looked at him. They did not know what to say and became more and more embarrassed. When Herr Mauch knocked on the door they both stood up at the same time and blushed crimson. Then they stepped out quickly between the beds, met in a clumsy embrace, and kissed each other.

PAUL ALVERDES was a German writer and dramatist, born in Strasbourg in 1897. He was the son of an army sergeant who had published his own account of his experience of war. Alverdes was a member of the German youth movement, and at the age of just 17, he enlisted voluntarily just weeks after the outbreak of World War I. While on the Western Front, he was severely injured in the throat on the Somme. He spent several years recovering in hospital. This type of injury features in several of his works.

He began studying law at university, but then changed to study German and art history. He then settled in Munich where he worked as a freelance writer, also undertaking translation.

His book *Die Pfeiferstube* (*The Whistlers' Room*) was first published in Frankfurt in 1929, and sold over a quarter of a million copies over the next two decades.

Many of his other works also centred on the experience of soldiers. In *Reinhold Oder Die Verwandelten* (*Reinhold at the Front*, published as part of the collection *Changed Men*), Alverdes describes the mortally wounded Reinhold, bound for a field hospital, choosing to return to his battery, to die there surrounded by his comrades.

In 1934, Alverdes and Benno von Mechow founded *Das Innere Reich*, which was the most important literary magazine officially published in Hitler's Germany. Though Alverdes did align himself with the struggle for the restoration of Germany's prestige, the magazine was controversial, and did publish a range of opinions, including pieces by writers who did not openly support the aims of the Third Reich.

Alverdes began writing for children in the late 1930s, publishing books and audio plays, and also adapting German folk tales. He died in Munich in 1979.

D R EMILY MAYHEW is a military medical historian specialising in the study of severe casualty, its infliction, treatment and long-term outcomes in 20th and 21st century warfare. She is historian in residence in the Department of Bioengineering, working primarily with the researchers and staff of The Royal British Legion Centre for Blast Injury Studies, and a Research Fellow in the Division of Surgery within the Department of Surgery and Cancer. She is based jointly in the Department of Bioengineering and at the Chelsea and Westminster campus. She is the author of *The Reconstruction of Warriors, Wounded: From Battlefield to Blighty, 1914–1918* and *A Heavy Reckoning: Life, Death and Survival in Afghanistan and beyond, 2007–2014.*

Mr Britling lives in the quintessentially English town of Matching's Easy in Essex. He is a great thinker, an essayist, but most of all an optimist. When war arrives he is forced to reassess many of the things he had been so sure of. The war brings great change – Belgian refugees come with dreadful stories and everywhere it seems there are young men dressed in khaki. The family's young German tutor is forced to head back to Germany, and Mr Britling's seventeen-year-old son enlists in the Territorials. Day by day and month by month, Wells chronicles the unfolding events and public reaction as witnessed by the inhabitants of one house in rural England.

Written in 1916 when the outcome of the war was still uncertain, the semi-autobiographical *Mr Britling Sees it Through* is a fascinating portrait of Britain at war and an insight into Wells' own ideals.

August 2016 | ISBN 9781612004150

MR BRITLING
SEES IT THROUGH

H. G. Wells

PASS GUARD
AT YPRES

Ronald Gurner

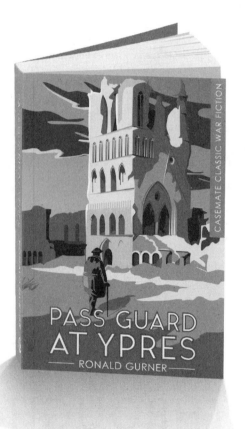

A platoon of inexperienced British soldiers crosses to France in excited and nervous anticipation of what is to come. They find themselves at Ypres where the battle-weary Allied troops are dug in, surrounded by slaughter. With their young, upright officer Freddy Mann, they are soon in the thick of it, burying the dead, suffering the terror of bombardment, and being picked off by snipers. The action unfolds through the soldiers' eyes, focusing on Freddy Mann's journey from idealistic officer fresh from school to battle-hardened cynic. Barely hanging on as those around him are killed, maimed and traumatised, Freddy suffers a crisis of faith, losing his belief in both the war and in everything he once stood for.

August 2016 | ISBN 9781612004112